Top 10 Dinosaurs of 2014

An  Book

By Sabrina Ricci

For Dinosaur Enthusiasts

Are you really into dinosaurs? Sign up to the I Know Dino mailing list (iknowdino.com) for news, updates, and special offers on all upcoming dinosaur books.

Top 10 Dinosaurs of 2014: An "I Know Dino" Book

This book is a blend of fiction and fact.

Published by I Know Dino, LLC

ISBN: 1622000161
ISBN-13: 978-1-62200-016-6

Dedicated to all dinosaur enthusiasts

Contents

Introduction

We live in a golden age of dinosaur discoveries, which is a wonderful time to be a dinosaur enthusiast.[1]

In 2014, at least 14 dinosaurs made the news.[2] They were a mix of newly described and published species, as well as new studies of species paleontologists had known existed for years but had known virtually nothing about.

Although we may never know exactly how dinosaurs lived and behaved, it's fun to dream up scenes of dinosaurs eating, fighting, and playing. And so, as a dinosaur enthusiast, inspired by dinosaur fiction such as *Raptor Red* by Dr. Robert T. Bakker and scenes in Dr. Anthony J. Martin's *Dinosaurs Without Bones*, I wrote *Top 10 Dinosaurs of 2014*.

The book is a mix of imagination and research, combining fictitious scenes of 10 of the dinosaurs that made headlines in 2014 with a list of facts about each one to help paint a broader picture. And, if you are interested in learning more about the dinosaurs in this book, check out the I Know Dino podcast.[3]

---

[1] http://www.buzzfeed.com/sricci/are-you-a-dinosaur-enthusiast-43-signs-youare-o-1lvel

[2] http://iknowdino.com/2014-dinosaur-discoveries/

[3] http://apple.co/1J4RuY6

Please enjoy.

—**Sabrina**

Anzu wyliei: "Chicken from Hell"

Anzu wyliei, courtesy of Scott Hartman, Lamanna MC, Sues H-D,
Schachner ER, and Lyson TR via Wikimedia Commons

All around is the sound of life. Bubbling, squawking,
growling, chomping, noisy life.

Anzu wyliei runs through it all, at a fast pace, avoiding the pockets of water in the wet floodplains he calls home. At 11 feet long, and weighing 500 or so pounds, *Anzu wyliei* is large enough to roam almost as freely as he would like. However, he does have to keep watch for *T. rex* in the area.

But today, *Anzu wyliei* is feeling carefree, enjoying the wind that ripples through his feathers on his upper arms as he moves swiftly. He holds his head up high, showing off the large, thin, bony crest that sits atop his head.

As *Anzu* runs, a female *Anzu* catches his eye. Intrigued, *Anzu* stops, using his long tail to help balance. He cocks his head at the female in a curious and an inviting way.

The female is not interested and turns her back on *Anzu*. But *Anzu* is not discouraged. He takes slow steps towards the female, careful not to scare her away. Eventually *Anzu* gets right next to her.

She continues to ignore him and uses her toothless beak to pick at some vegetation on the ground. *Anzu* does the same, using his sliding jaw joint to cut up the plants. After each bite, he lifts his head to steal another glance at her.

Then he notices a small, unsuspecting animal nearby. *Anzu* is quick to use his beak and claws to grab hold of his prey and cut into it. The prey squirms but is no match for *Anzu*. Once it goes limp, *Anzu* nudges the meat towards the female, who inspects *Anzu* more closely.

Anzu tilts his head so she can better see his tall crest. But the gesture annoys her, and she backs away, giving *Anzu* a warning sound. *Anzu* decides to take the aggressive approach and moves a step closer.

Another male *Anzu* comes from nearby and charges *Anzu*. *Anzu*, too immersed in impressing the female and not expecting competition, is caught off guard as the other male knocks the wind out of him. *Anzu* quickly recovers and switches from mating to fighting mode.

He spreads out his arms and runs towards the other male. But the other male is prepared and pecks at *Anzu*'s head, taking a small chunk of skin off the top. Angry, *Anzu* jumps and kicks the other male. He can hear a crack, and the other male yelps in pain and falls, clutching his ribs.

Cocky, *Anzu* struts towards the female, who now looks at him with interest. But he stands too close to the other male, who, with one last burst of energy, thrusts himself onto *Anzu*'s foot and latches on with his beak.

Anzu struggles and pulls himself away with all his might. But the other male has surprising strength and holds his grip, causing *Anzu*'s tendon to be ripped away from his toe bone.

Anzu screeches in pain and limps away, no longer caring about the female. He gets as far away as he can before collapsing and tending to his wound.

Facts about *Anzu wyliei*

- *Anzu wyliei* was an oviraptorosaur that lived in the Late Cretaceous in what is now North and South Dakota, U.S.
- *Anzu* was bird-like, with a long tail, and had a sliding jaw joint that may have been used to eat plants and meat. Two of the three *Anzu* specimens discovered had injuries, one with a broken and healed rib and the other with an arthritic toe bone.
- According to Dr. Hans-Dieter Sues, co-author of the *Anzu* study, and his team, though climate change may have contributed to dinosaurs going extinct, *Anzu* proves that dinosaurs were still evolving and were diverse end at the end.
- The genus name *Anzu* refers to an ancient Mesopotamiam feathered demon.
- The species name *wyliei* is in honor of Wylie J. Tuttle, a dinosaur enthusiast and the grandson of Mr. and Mrs. Foster, who have contributed to the Carnegie Museum of Natural History.

 *Find out more in the* I Know Dino *podcast, episode 17, "Anzu."*

Aquilops americanus:
"American Eagle Face"

Aquilops americanus, courtesy of Brian Engh via Wikimedia Commons

From high overhead, no one can see the tiny dinosaur perusing the plants on the ground. Weighing only 3.5 pounds and measuring 24 inches long, *Aquilops*—one of the smallest dinosaurs—snips off plants with his hook-like beak.

But none of the ferns or saplings nearby are of interest. *Aquilops* doesn't mind foraging. He has just spent the last few months with his herd, walking across the last piece of the Bering Strait toward what will be known as North America, and his new home. It took multiple generations for his herd to make it to North America from Asia, and *Aquilops* hopes it was worthwhile.

The journey had been long and daunting, and not everyone made it. But *Aquilops* never gave up hope, and the thought of new, tasty food keeps him going. So he doesn't mind walking a little further in search for vegetation.

Aquilops walks on two legs, his long tail helping to keep his balance. On two legs, he can move faster and, although *Aquilops* hasn't quite found the perfect meal yet, he is getting hungry.

Deciding to change course, *Aquilops* bends down, using the prong on his rostral bone to dig for food. At first, nothing good comes up. Then *Aquilops*'s prong hits a root. Curious, *Aquilops* cuts off a piece and tastes it.

The root has a sweet flavor and hits the spot. *Aquilops* digs to find more, grunting with pleasure.

Soon other *Aquilopses* join the little dinosaur. But *Aquilops* is not willing to share with his herd. He stops digging and moves to cover the spot in the ground where he found the tasty root. He grunts, this time as a warning.

Most of the others back away, not willing to fight over an unknown plant. But one stays behind. She shuffles her feet, ready to attack.

Aquilops gets angry. He found the food first; he should not have to share. He lowers his head, preparing to strike.

After a few moments, the two dinosaurs run at each other. They hit one another with their prongs.

Aquilops feels the sting of the first blow, but that only fuels his anger. He moves backwards a couple of steps, only to run forward again, this time with greater momentum.

The female *Aquilops* is ready and braces herself for the impact. But *Aquilops* has much more force than he anticipated and, this time, part of the female's beak breaks. The pain is so intense that she cries out and quickly shuffles away.

Proud, *Aquilops* returns triumphantly to his meal. He digs into the roots without any hesitation, savoring every bite. The months of walking and struggling for this meal were worth it. This new land will give *Aquilops* a lot of opportunities, and he looks forward to digging up other new plants.

Though *Aquilops* is a juvenile, he will not grow much bigger. But he will lay the groundwork for bigger descendants. About 40 million years into the future, *Triceratops*—one of the most famous ceratopsians—will walk through the same area. Unlike *Aquilops*, *Triceratops* will have horns and a neck frill. And it will be 4,000 times bigger.

Facts about *Aquilops americanus*

- *Aquilops americanus* was a ceratopsian that lived in the Early Cretaceous in what is now southern Montana, U.S.
- Only the skull of *Aquilops* has been found. But the team that found *Aquilops* determined how the rest of its body looked based on the bodies of close relatives.
- *Aquilops* came from Asia, probably crossing the Bering Strait. It is more closely related to Asian dinosaurs than North American ones.
- *Aquilops* had a hook-like beak and a prong on its rostral bone, which forms its upper, parrot-like beak and may have been used for fighting or digging.

- The name *Aquilops americanus* means "American eagle face"; the genus name *Aquilops* comes from its hook-like beak.

 *Find out more in the* I Know Dino *podcast, episode 13, "Aquilops."*

Changyuraptor yangi:

"Long-feathered robber"

Changyuraptor yangi, courtesy of Emily Willoughby via Wikimedia Commons

The breeze feels cool and refreshing, ruffling the feathers on *Changyuraptor yangi*'s body. Gliding through the dense trees is the most natural thing in the world, and *Changyuraptor* relishes the tall obstacles, using the feathers on her legs and tail to turn quickly and avoid colliding with branches.

The view is beautiful. Below, *Changyuraptor* can see other animals stuck on the ground. A terrible way to live, she thinks. One of those animals is *Yutyrannus*, busy ripping open its prey with its sharp, menacing teeth. *Yutyrannus* is a fearsome predator, also covered in feathers. *Changyuraptor* is glad that the tyrannosaur cannot fly.

Changyuraptor moves higher into the air and turns to get a view of the volcanoes. They are large and menacing. But, in the sky, *Changyuraptor* feels safe. Nearby is a lake. *Changyuraptor* salivates at the thought of the fish and frogs that live in the water.

But the wind is blowing in the right direction, and *Changyuraptor* decides to ignore the potential prey for now and stay in the sky. The day is warm and sunny, and she would rather spend time in the air. She lowers herself back among the trees, taking care to twist and turn.

Changyuraptor spreads out her full 21-foot wingspan and brushes past a tree with long branches and thick, bundled leaves. The edges of the leaves scrape against *Changyuraptor*, but she doesn't mind. She continues to glide around the trees.

From the corner of her eye, *Changyuraptor* sees a sudden movement. A small lizard scurries up a conifer tree. *Changyuraptor* salivates. Lunch.

She swivels and dives towards the lizard, using her tail feathers to slow down at the last second and land on the ground, near the trunk of the tree. But the lizard is also quick and jumps away before *Changyuraptor* has a chance to catch her prey.

Frustrated, *Changyuraptor* decides to move on. She grabs onto the tree and pulls herself up, climbing further and further until she reaches nearly the top. She hops over to a slightly taller tree next to it and continues to climb. *Changyuraptor* is a great climber and enjoys the exercise. It's almost as good as flying.

Up here, *Changyuraptor* sees a small bird, flying at a slow speed, not too far away. Her stomach growls, and she jumps and heads towards the bird. The bird hears *Changyuraptor* and starts to move faster. But *Changyuraptor* is determined not to miss another meal. Using all four of her wings, *Changyuraptor* quickly catches up to the bird and attacks.

The bird tries to find cover in the trees, but *Changyuraptor* is too nimble. After just a few seconds, *Changyuraptor* has her lunch. Satisfied, she lands and rips into her prey. The meat is warm and, after *Changyuraptor* gets her fill, she walks briskly to a nearby tree and begins climbing.

When she reaches the top, she notices a *Yutyrannus* walk by.

Good choice, *Changyuraptor* thinks. It is always safer to be higher up.

Facts about *Changyuraptor yangi*

- *Changyuraptor yangi* was a dromaeosaur that lived in the Cretaceous period in what is now northeastern China.
- *Changyuraptor* had long leg feathers that looked like a second set of wings.
- *Changyuraptor* is not a bird but is instead a non-avian dinosaur that could probably fly and/or glide.
- Paleontologists still don't know exactly how *Changyuraptor* moved through the air. But *Changyuraptor* could probably turn and brake fast through dense trees.
- *The genus name Changyuraptor* means "long-feathered robber."

 *Find out more in the* I Know Dino *podcast, episode 22, "Changyuraptor."*

Deinocheirus mirificus:
"Terrible Hand"

Deinocheirus mirificus, courtesy of FunkMonk (Michael B. H.)
via Wikimedia Commons

The sun is hot on *Deinocheirus mirificus*'s back. The morning had passed quickly and uneventfully. *Deinocheirus* wades in a shallow stream, partly to find food, but mostly to cool himself down. His hoof-like claws on his toes keep him from sinking in the mud.

The dinosaur lowers his head towards the water and, with his duck-like bill, *Deinocheirus* sucks up the soft plants that hide at the bottom of the stream. His round, flat beak is covered in keratin, which strengthens it. *Deinocheirus* uses his big tongue inside his deep, lower jaw to push the vegetation down his gullet. *Deinocheirus* has no teeth so, to help grind up his meal, *Deinocheirus* picks up a couple of smooth stones and swallows them whole. These gastroliths will help him digest food over time.

A small fish swims near *Deinocheirus* to pick at the plants. Not wanting to miss an opportunity, *Deinocheirus* reaches out for the fish with his 8-foot-long arms. The fish tries to dart out of the way, but *Deinocheirus* uses his claws to catch the prey. The giant dinosaur has a weak bite, so he cannot simply take a chunk out of his meal. Instead, *Deinocheirus* scoops up the fish from his hands with his tongue and swallows.

Now, after a light snack and a chance to cool down, *Deinocheirus* wades out of the water and looks for more vegetation to eat. At 35 feet long and weighing 6 tons, he lumbers out of the water on his two muscular legs and heads for a patch of trees full of fresh, mouth-watering leaves.

Deinocheirus pulls down the branches with his claws and plucks off his food. With his long, ostrich-like neck, he can reach almost all of the vegetation. As he eats, *Deinocheirus*'s tail feathers wag happily. He is so engrossed in his food that he almost doesn't see the hungry *Tarbosaurus* approach.

But he hears the carnivore growl and, though *Deinocheirus* is not the brightest dinosaur, he understands that he is in danger. Instincts kick in, and *Deinocheirus* looks around for an escape route. But *Tarbosaurus* is too close and *Deinocheirus* has too large a stomach and cannot run, so he must find another way to defend himself.

Deinocheirus decides to make himself seem bigger. He lifts his large, horse-like head and straightens out his s-curved back, to better emphasize the sail-like structure that lines his vertebrae. He grunts to show *Tarbosaurus* that he is not afraid.

Tarbosaurus takes a closer look at *Deinocheirus*, sizing him up. Puffed up, *Deinocheirus* looks much bigger than *Tarbosaurus* originally thinks. Eventually, the carnivore decides that it is not worth the effort and backs away.

Deinocheirus waits for the predator to skulk out of sight, and then resumes eating. Wanting to spice up his diet, he chooses to dig for the next meal, using his blunt claws to root for food in the ground.

The fish and the plants are not enough for *Deinocheirus*, and he wants to eat as much as he can before the sun sets and he must settle in for the night.

Facts about *Deinocheirus mirificus*

- *Deinocheirus mirificus* was an ornithomimosaur that lived in the Cretaceous in what is now Mongolia's Gobi Desert.
- *Deinocheirus* was originally discovered in 1965. But, for 50 years, all scientists knew about *Deinocheirus* was that it had giant, 8-foot-long arms.
- *Deinocheirus* had spines like *Spinosaurus*; truncated, hoof-like claws on its feet; an ostrich-like neck; a flat, duck-like bill; a large lower jaw; tail feathers; short claws on its hands; bulky, tyrannosaur-like hind legs; and sauropod-like hips.
- *Deinocheirus* has been compared to Jar Jar Binks from *Star Wars* because it looks so strange.
- The genus name *Deinocheirus* means "terrible hand."

 *Find out more in the* I Know Dino *podcast, episode 10, "Deinocheirus."*

Dreadnoughtus schrani:

"Fear nothing"

Thud. Thud. Thud. Thud.

The trees shake as the 85-foot-long *Dreadnoughtus schrani*—one of the biggest dinosaurs to ever live—moves a few feet to a new grazing spot.

He lets his 65-ton frame settle in, the ground spongy and soft and sinking under the weight. At 30 feet tall, and with a 37-foot-long neck, *Dreadnoughtus* can see for miles. He is happy with what he sees: enough vegetation to eat for many hours, possibly days. Not too far away is a lake, which *Dreadnoughtus* plans to visit later for a drink. From a short distance, the lake looks full and sparkling; the water is clear.

Dreadnoughtus is still a growing dinosaur, and he needs to eat at least half a ton of food every day to sustain himself. The juvenile strips the surrounding leaves with his cylindrical, 1-inch-long teeth, swallowing his food whole.

The process delights *Dreadnoughtus*, who plans to spend the next four hours in this same spot. His stomach is like a bottomless pit, and he never feels quite full. But spending the day eating makes him happy.

Dreadnoughtus keeps his neck horizontal as he eats. The day is warm, but *Dreadnoughtus* has air sacs inside his tail to help keep him cool.

Below the trees, younger, smaller *Dreadnoughtuses* run around, scrambling to eat as much food as possible while staying out of sight of predators. They are not yet big enough to defend themselves. But they are big enough to catch the larger *Dreadnoughtus*'s eye.

Annoyed, the larger juvenile *Dreadnoughtus* flexes his claws on his back feet. He has staked out this area for himself and will not tolerate others eating his food. The claws are sharp and long. The smaller *Dreadnoughtuses* take the warning seriously and move away.

Satisfied, *Dreadnoughtus* returns to stripping and swallowing leaves. The ground starts to shake. Confused, *Dreadnoughtus* looks down but cannot tell what is happening. Everything below is moving, and *Dreadnoughtus* can feel his body vibrating, but he knows he is standing still.

After a few seconds, the shaking stops.

When *Dreadnoughtus* looks back up, he sees the water from the nearby lake, now in the form of a large wave, rushing towards him.

Unsure of what to do, *Dreadnoughtus* decides to stand his ground. He plants his feet more firmly in the ground, digging his claws into the dirt and bracing for the water to hit.

The water rushes towards the dinosaur quickly, sweeping away smaller dinosaurs and crushing trees in its path.

But *Dreadnoughtus* is not afraid. He is large and confident that he can survive. But he is aggravated that he has to pause his eating for this inconvenience.

The water hits *Dreadnoughtus* with such a force that it nearly knocks over the dinosaur. The first impact reaches the base of his neck, but soon more water hits.

Dreadnoughtus feels cold but manages to keep his footing—for now. More and more water comes, each time higher than before. *Dreadnoughtus* raises his head as high as he can, but it's not enough. The water keeps coming.

Facts about *Dreadnoughtus schrani*

- *Dreadnoughtus schrani* was a titanosaur that lived in the Late Cretaceous in what is now Argentina.
- Dr. Kenneth Lacovara and his team discovered 45 percent of a complete *Dreadnoughtus* skeleton during excavations in Argentina between 2005 and 2009.
- The dinosaur was so big that it probably had no predators.
- *Dreadnoughtus* had such a large stomach that its food would have stayed undigested for months.
- The genus name *Dreadnoughtus* means "fear nothing"; the species name *schrani* comes from Adam Schran, who helped fund the research.

 *Find out more in the* I Know Dino *podcast, episode 9, "Dreadnoughtus."*

Kulindadromeus zabaikalicus:
"Kulinda River running dinosaur"

Kulindadromeus zabaikalicus, courtesy of Tomopteryx via Wikimedia Commons

Wind slices through *Kulindadromeus zabaikalicus*'s feathers as he runs as fast as his two small legs can carry him. Although *Kulindadromeus* is only 5 feet long, the little dinosaur is known in his habitat for his speed.

The wind feels good. But, after a few minutes, *Kulindadromeus* slows down and stops to take a drink from the river near where he lives. From the edge of the water, he has a good view of one of the many volcanoes in the area. They are all active, but *Kulindadromeus* has adapted to life near the volcanoes and knows how to get away when necessary.

He takes a few steps into the water and splashes around. The water weighs down the feathers on his arms and legs, but *Kulindadromeus* doesn't care. The day is warm and the extra insulation is a burden, at least for now. When night falls, the down feathers will be more welcome.

After his thirst is quenched and *Kulindadromeus* has cooled down, he leaves the water and searches for food. Vegetation lies only a few feet away, but it is tough plant matter. Fortunately, *Kulindadromeus* has sharp ridges in his teeth to help him chew. He bites into his lunch with gusto, loudly chewing with his mouth open.

The vegetation is rough, but the scales on *Kulindadromeus*'s hands, ankles, and feet help protect the dinosaur and prevent cuts. *Kulindadromeus* also has scales on his tail, which he uses for balance while he bites off vegetation.

Sensing another dinosaur, the bristles on *Kulindadromeus*'s head and back stiffen. *Kulindadromeus* takes a break from his lunch and turns around.

A female *Kulindadromeus* awaits him. Though *Kulindadromeus* is still a juvenile, he is old enough to know how his kind mates. Wanting to impress the female, he uses his short arms to show off his impressive, soft feathers.

The female, who is also young, seems to approve. Slowly she approaches *Kulindadromeus* but is interrupted when the nearby volcano erupts. The eruption is sudden, and ash and lava spew out thousands of feet into the air, accompanied by a deafening roar. Ash and dust form a large, dark cloud that starts to roll towards the dinosaurs.

Kulindadromeus can see rocks falling. He quickly looks over to the female, and they give each other a curt nod before taking off. Lava could start flowing at any moment, and it is best to get away as far as possible.

Kulindadromeus flaps his arms, but he cannot fly. Instead, both *Kulindadromeus* and the female *Kulindadromeus* run as fast as they can. Behind them, the smoke and ash gobble up everything, covering it in darkness.

The two run for miles, not stopping to look back. They head uphill when they can. Eventually, they can no longer run, and they collapse. Luckily, the volcano's eruption is relatively small, and they are out of harm's way.

After stopping to catch his breath, *Kulindadromeus* looks over at the female. She feels him staring, and she looks back at him. He raises his arms, so she can once again see his impressive feathers.

Facts about *Kulindadromeus zabaikalicus*

- *Kulindadromeus zabaikalicus* was a neornithischian that lived in the Jurassic in what is now eastern Siberia.
- *Kulindadromeus* is one of the few herbivores found to have fossil feathers, which makes some scientists believe that all dinosaurs could have had feathers, or at least the potential for feathers.
- The area where *Kulindadromeus* was found had a lot of volcanoes. Fossil feathers are rare, and they may be preserved in *Kulindadromeus* because the dinosaur specimens fell to the bottom of the nearby lake and were covered in ash.
- *Kulindadromeus* could not fly, but it may have used its feathers for insulation or display.
- The genus name *Kulindadromeus* means "Kulinda runner." *Kulindadromeus* was found near the Kulinda River.

 *Find out more in the I Know Dino podcast, episode 12, "Kulindadromeus."*

Nanuqsaurus hoglundi:

"Polar bear lizard"

Nanuqsaurus hoglundi, courtesy of Tomopteryx via Wikimedia
Commons

Among the tall conifer trees and flowering plants along the coast, a top predator looks for her dinner. The sun has started to set.

Nanuqsaurus hoglundi is not that large: only 20-feet long and weighing 1,000 pounds. But she is still the top predator in the Arctic subcontinent Larimidia where she lives—partly because of her powerful bite.

The days are getting shorter, which means winter is coming. And *Nanuqsaurus* knows that she must find easy meals while she still can.

Life in the Arctic is difficult, though not because of the weather. Temperatures dip but never get so cold that *Nanuqsaurus* cannot walk around. The fuzz that covers her body also helps keep her warm.

But, in the winter season, the nights get longer and longer, sometimes lasting a full 24 hours. In addition to being hard to see, *Nanuqsaurus* knows that the prey she usually hunts will either migrate elsewhere or hide away and sleep for the next few months.

Nanuqsaurus sniffs around for signs of prey. She has a long nasal cavity and a strong sense of smell, which is especially useful in the dark. After a few moments, she gets a whiff of a herd of hadrosaurs not too far away.

She salivates at the thought. *Nanuqsaurus* quickly catches up to the herd. They are starting to head south. In big groups they are dangerous, but alone they are weak and not that bright.

Nanuqsaurus knows that she must separate one from the herd—one that is frail or small. She decides that the best way to do this is to scare them by making her presence known. The carnivore roars as loudly as she can to attract attention. It works.

Scared and confused, the hadrosaurs start to run but in different directions. *Nanuqsaurus* takes her time and watches, looking for her best opportunity. Then she spots a juvenile hadrosaur. The prey brays, unhappy and afraid. *Nanuqsaurus* springs into action.

She starts running for the herbivore, jaws open and ready to bite, flashing her killer whale-like teeth.

The hadrosaur sees the carnivore coming, kicks into high gear, and runs away. It heads towards where the majority of the herd is running, but it cannot catch up in time.

Nanuqsaurus pounces, and bites down hard into the hadrosaur. It whimpers, as *Nanuqsaurus*'s teeth tear into its flesh. Eventually the hadrosaur bleeds out and stops making sounds.

In a few short weeks, it will not be this easy to find food, so *Nanuqsaurus* knows that she must enjoy it while it lasts. Life in the North is not easy and, though *Nanuqsaurus* is fairly small—especially compared to her cousins *T.rex* and *Tarbosaurus*—and has adapted to her habitat, the long months before summer are difficult to survive.

It will take a lot of skill to sniff out food sources and successfully hunt them.

For now, *Nanuqsaurus* enjoys the warmth of the blood and relishes every morsel. She uses her twiggy arms to help her balance as she digs in.

Facts about *Nanuqsaurus hoglundi*

- *Nanuqsaurus hoglundi* was a tyrannosaur that lived in the Cretaceous in what is now Alaska, U.S.
- *Nanuqsaurus* lived in the Arctic, 70 million years ago, but enjoyed weather that was similar to modern-day Seattle.
- *The Arctic in Nanuqsaurus'* lifetime was warm, with lots of tall trees and flowering plants, though it did have extra-long days in the summer and sometimes 24 hours of darkness in the winter.
- *Nanuqsaurus* had a great sense of smell, which would have been useful in winter when it was dark.

- The genus name *Nanuqsaurus* means "polar bear lizard."

 *Find out more in the* I Know Dino *podcast, episode 11, "Nanuqsaurus."*

Qianzhousaurus sinensis:
"Pinocchio rex"

Qianzhousaurus sinensis shuffles through the lush trees along the edge of a body of water. At 29 feet long and weighing 1,800 pounds, she is one of the fiercest and most threatening dinosaurs in the area.

At first glance, she doesn't look too threatening, with her comically long, thin snout covered in tiny horns. But the other inhabitants know better. Nearby, an oviraptor busies itself by crushing a mollusk in the water. Soon it senses *Qianzhousaurus*, and it jerks its head up, leaves the mollusk, and runs in the opposite direction.

Qianzhousaurus grunts, flashing her long, narrow teeth. The oviraptor is too far away to see. Not discouraged, *Qianzhousaurus* takes softer steps, keeping an eye out for a quick meal.

Soon *Qianzhousaurus* spots a small lizard. She starts to stalk her prey, careful not to alert it to any danger. When *Qianzhousaurus* is within striking distance, she traps the lizard with her feet. The lizard reacts too late and tries to wriggle free, but *Qianzhousaurus* is strong and heavy.

Salivating, *Qianzhousaurus* crushes her prey and leans down to take a bite. She swallows a small chunk, and then takes the rest in her teeth, tilting her head back so that the carcass falls into her mouth. It's a small piece of meat, but it's warm and easily slides down *Qianzhousaurus*'s gullet.

Still hungry, *Qianzhousaurus* glances around, looking for another easy target. A sauropod catches *Qianzhousaurus*'s eye, but *Qianzhousaurus* knows that she does not have a strong enough bite to take down such a large creature. *Qianzhousaurus* feels the sauropod eyeing her, watching her, but it's too far away to get into a fight.

Qianzhousaurus turns her eyes in a different direction. She hears a splash from behind and rotates to see the source of the sound.

Another oviraptor.

Qianzhousaurus thinks she has a chance of catching this one, but she knows she will have to be quick. From the corner of her eye, she sees another *Qianzhousaurus*, joining her in the hunt. *Qianzhousaurus* makes brief eye contact with her kin, giving her approval.

The two predators chase after the oviraptor, who is slowed down by the water. *Qianzhousaurus* and her partner move along on either side of their prey. Scared, the oviraptor looks from side to side, judging which way to go next.

Qianzhousaurus braces herself. If the oviraptor heads in her direction, *Qianzhousaurus* will need a burst of speed to take it down.

The oviraptor leaps out of the water and dashes as fast as it can in front of the other *Qianzhousaurus*, who is not prepared and stumbles.

Qianzhousaurus lets out a roar and runs through the shallow water towards the oviraptor, nearly knocking over the other *Qianzhousaurus*.

She is fast and almost catches up to the oviraptor. But the oviraptor is just a little bit faster. As a final attempt, *Qianzhousaurus* stretches out her neck and chomps at the oviraptor, hoping to reach it with her long snout. But all she gets is a mouth full of feathers.

Frustrated, *Qianzhousaurus* stops and spits them out. She will have to find another meal.

Facts about *Qianzhousaurus sinensis*

- *Qianzhousaurus sinensis* was a tyrannosaurid that lived in the Cretaceous in what is now China.
- According to the study's leader Junchang Lu from the Chinese Academy of Geological Sciences in Beijing, the *Qianzhousaurus* skeleton was so complete because, right after it died, dirt buried it, which protected it from water and air eroding it.
- *Qianzhousaurus* had a snout 35 percent longer than other dinosaurs of its size. *Qianzhousaurus* got its nickname, "Pinocchio rex," because of its long snout.
- Scientists do not yet know what *Qianzhousaurus* used its nose for, but they plan on using computer models to see how *Qianzhousaurus* used its snout. Modern animals with long snouts, like crocodiles, use them to catch fish.
- The genus name *Qianzhousaurus* comes from Qianzhou, the ancient name for the Chinese city Ganzhou, where a nearly complete *Qianzhousaurus* specimen was found.

 *Find out more in the* I Know Dino *podcast, episode 19, "Qianzhousaurus."*

Spinosaurus aegyptiacus: "Spiny Lizard"

Spinosaurus aegyptiacus, courtesy of ДиБгд via Wikimedia Commons

The water is murky. Sand and grit stir it up, making it difficult for the giant predator with the 6-foot-tall sail on his back to see. He lowers his mouth into the water, his high nostrils allowing him to breathe easily while the pits on his snout feel for pressure and sense for fish swimming nearby.

Nothing moves, or at least nothing worth attempting to catch. The large theropod—*Spinosaurus aegyptiacus*—wades into the water. Tired from balancing his long head and neck with his short back legs, *Spinosaurus* relaxes as he submerges like a crocodile, flexing his flat, webbed feet in the water.

The river is shallow, but *Spinosaurus* paddles quietly, looking for easy prey. An unsuspecting sawfish passes by. It is 25 feet long with jagged teeth.

Spinosaurus knows the sawfish will be hard to catch, but the thought of a big meal is enticing. He opens his mouth and tries to rake in the fish with his teeth. Needle-like teeth line the sides of his upper jaw, with more teeth behind them and interlocking teeth at the end of his snout. *Spinosaurus* tries to bite down with his powerful jaw, but his teeth are not serrated, so he cannot just rip apart the sawfish.

The teeth land in the wrong place, near the sawfish's narrow rostrum, which has sharp teeth along it, like a saw. The sawfish struggles, its teeth digging into *Spinosaurus*. *Spinosaurus* shakes his long, narrow head and tries to at least stun the sawfish, so he can eat it without the struggle.

But the sawfish proves to be too strong, and *Spinosaurus* is forced to let go. The sawfish swims away as fast as it can while *Spinosaurus* tends to his wounds. The cuts aren't too deep, and *Spinosaurus* is not that hurt, but he feels the sting of defeat in the pit of his empty stomach.

Back on the surface, *Spinosaurus* keeps only his nostrils above water while he paddles towards land. Only his sail and two large eyes can be seen.

A pterosaur lands at the edge of the water and stops to take a drink. *Spinosaurus* spots the potential meal. Still hungry, *Spinosaurus* decides to scare and confuse his prey.

Spinosaurus raises his sail to create a shadow in the water, arching his back for effect. It works.

The pterosaur continues to sip but more cautiously. *Spinosaurus* slowly moves towards his prey. When he gets within biting distance, he opens his jaws and snaps down quickly. But not quickly enough.

The pterosaur flaps its wings and, with a surge of adrenaline, manages to get away, though not without a souvenir. When the pterosaur fights its way out of *Spinosaurus*'s jaws, it rips out one of *Spinosaurus*'s teeth.

The pterosaur is badly wounded and dripping blood, which only makes *Spinosaurus* hungrier. He lunges out of the water and runs for the injured prey, using his arms as legs. When he gets close, he reaches out with his blade-like claws, grasping for the pterosaur.

But his stumpy back legs and front-heavy top get in the way. *Spinosaurus* stumbles and the pterosaur flees, escaping for good this time.

Stomach growling, *Spinosaurus* returns to the water where he lies in wait for an easier kill.

Facts about *Spinosauru aegyptiacus*

- *Spinosaurus aegyptiacus* was a spinosaurid that lived in the Late Cretaceous in what is now North Africa.
- *Spinosaurus* had a sail that it may have used for thermoregulation, to create shadows to find prey, or to attract mates.
- *Spinosaurus* was first discovered in 1912, but the first *Spinosaurus* fossils found were destroyed in World War II.
- New fossils were eventually found, and *Spinosaurus* was described in a new study published in 2014.
- The genus name *Spinosaurus* means "spiny lizard."

 *Find out more in the I Know Dino podcast, episode 6, "Spinosaurus."*

Torvosaurus gurneyi:

"Savage lizard"

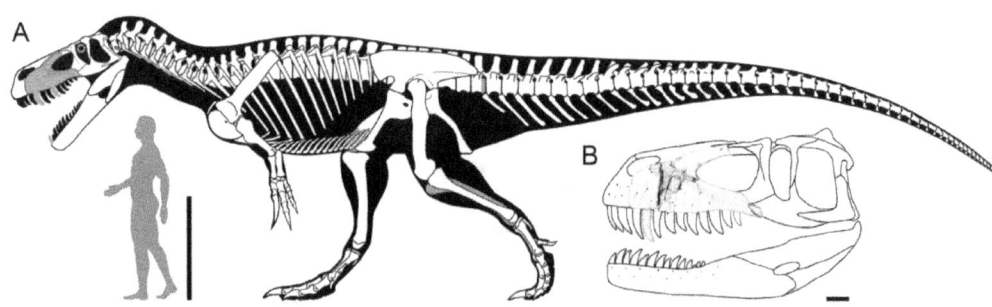

Torvosaurus gurneyi, courtesy of Scott Hartman, Carol Abraczinskas, Simão Mateus, Christophe Hendrickx, and Octávio Mateus via Wikimedia Commons

The ground quivers as *Torvosaurus gurneyi* takes a step. Pebbles bounce off the earth when *Torvosaurus* takes another step. He stops to sniff the air.

Around him, *Torvosaurus* can feel the tension. Small dinosaurs scatter and run away, trying to blend in with the lush vegetation. But *Torvosaurus* doesn't care; they are too small, and *Torvosaurus* has a craving for a larger meal.

At 32 feet long and weighing 4 to 5 tons, *Torvosaurus* is the largest predator in his habitat. His name, meaning "savage lizard," is accurate: *Torvosaurus* is equipped with sharp claws and 4-inch-long, blade-shaped teeth.

The air smells sweet and fresh, thanks to a large river that cuts through the middle of the vegetation. *Torvosaurus* lets his eyes wander; potential food sources are always more vulnerable when they are thirsty.

Torvosaurus is in luck. *Lusotitan* stands by the river, only a few yards away. The large sauropod is a formidable match for *Torvosaurus*, being 80 feet long and weighing 50 tons, but *Torvosaurus* is in the mood for a challenge. He just has to be careful of *Lusotitan*'s tail.

Torvosaurus walks quickly over to *Lusotitan*. He knows *Lusotitan* can hear him coming, so *Torvosaurus* prepares himself for the fight. When *Torvosaurus* gets within a few feet of *Lusotitan*, he stops and roars as loudly as he can, showing off his sharp teeth. He also flexes his claws for good measure.

Lusotitan growls back at *Torvosaurus* and lashes its tail. Their noises attract other, smaller carnivores' attention. Behind *Lusotitan,* *Torvosaurus* sees *Allosaurus*. *Allosaurus* is too far away to attack, but *Torvosaurus* can see that *Allosaurus* is interested. *Torvosaurus* knows that, if he wins this fight, he may have to defend his kill.

For now though, *Torvosaurus* turns his attention to *Lusotitan,* just as *Lusotitan* rears up on its hind legs. *Torvosaurus* sees a chance and is quick to step forward and take a large bite out of his prey.

The fight is over almost as soon as it starts.

Lusotitan yelps in pain and gets back on all fours. The blood drips, a heavy flow, but *Lusotitan* is still too strong for *Torvosaurus*. *Torvosaurus* backs away a few steps and waits for the blood loss to take its toll on his meal.

He has to wait a while, but *Torvosaurus* doesn't mind. Dizzy and weak, *Lusotitan* eventually falls to its side. *Torvosaurus* comes closer, and *Lusotitan* tries to snap at *Torvosaurus*. *Torvosaurus* roars and, with brute force, takes another large bite out of *Lusotitan*, this time out of the neck.

The meat is warm and already attracts other carnivores. *Torvosaurus* sees *Allosaurus* from earlier trying to sneak in and scavenge *Torvosaurus*'s kill. Angry, *Torvosaurus* runs at *Allosaurus,* biting at its heels. *Allosaurus* runs into the vegetation, far enough away where it knows that *Torvosaurus* will not follow—at least not while *Torvosaurus* is enjoying his meal.

Torvosaurus returns to *Lusotitan*'s carcass and rips out another chunk of flesh, satisfied.

Facts about *Torvosaurus guerneyi*

- *Torvosaurus guerneyi* was a megalosaurid that lived in the Late Jurassic in what is now Portugal.
- Christophe Hendrickx, who was a PhD student at the New University of Lisbon in Portugal, discovered *Torvosaurus gurneyi* when studying what scientists thought were the bones of *Torvosaurus tanneri,* a related species that lived in North America's Rocky Mountains in the Jurassic period.
- *Torvosaurus* probably hunted large prey, but may also have been a scavenger.
- The genus name *Torvosaurus* means "savage lizard."
- The species name *gurneyi* comes from the paleo-artist James Gurney, who created *Dinotopia* (published in 1992)..

Find out more in the I Know Dino *podcast, episode 16, "Torvosaurus."*

About the Author

 Sabrina is a writer and podcaster. She loves nerdy things, like technical specs and dinosaurs, especially sauropods. When she's not writing, she's podcasting with her husband at I Know Dino, a weekly show about dinosaurs.

I Know Dino (iknowdino.com), a weekly show about dinosaurs.

For Dinosaur Enthusiasts

Are you really into dinosaurs? Sign up to the I Know Dino mailing list (iknowdino.com) for news, updates, and special offers on all upcoming dinosaur books.

Connect With Sabrina via I Know Dino:

Website: iknowdino.com

iTunes: bitly.com/iknowdino

Instagram: instagram.com/iknowdino

YouTube: youtube.com/c/iknowdino

Facebook: facebook.com/iknowdino

Twitter: twitter.com/IKnowDino

TikTok: tiktok.com/@iknowdino

Pinterest: pinterest.com/iknowdino

Tumblr: http://iknowdino.tumblr.com

LinkedIn: linkedin.com/company/i-know-dino

Patreon: patreon.com/iknowdino

Resources

I Know Dino
   Website: http://iknowdino.com/
   Podcast: http://apple.co/1J4RuY6

Anzu wyliei

- http://journals.plos.org/plosone/article?id=10.1371/j
  ournal.pone.0092022
- http://www.smithsonianmag.com/smithsonian-
  institution/scientists-discover-discover-large-
  feathered-dinosaur-once-roamed-north-america-
  180950130/?no-ist

Aquilops americanus

- http://journals.plos.org/plosone/article?id=10.1371/j
  ournal.pone.0112055
- http://news.nationalgeographic.com/news/2014/12/1
  41210-ceratopsian-aquilops-dinosaur-fossil-
  paleontology-science/

Changyuraptor yangi

- http://www.nature.com/ncomms/2014/140715/ncom
  ms5382/full/ncomms5382.html
- http://www.livescience.com/46803-changyuraptor-
  yangi-dinosaur-longest-feathers.html

Deinocheirus mirificus

- http://www.nature.com/nature/journal/v515/n7526/full/nature13874.html
- http://phenomena.nationalgeographic.com/2014/10/22/deinocheirus-exposed-meet-the-body-behind-the-terrible-hand/

Dreadnoughtus schrani

- http://www.nature.com/articles/srep06196
- http://www.nytimes.com/2014/09/05/science/dinosaur-dreadnoughtus-discovery.html?_r=1

Kulindadromeus zabaikalicus

- http://www.sciencemag.org/content/345/6195/451.abstract
- http://news.nationalgeographic.com/news/2014/07/140724-feathered-siberia-dinosaur-scales-science/

Nanuqsaurus hoglundi

- http://journals.plos.org/plosone/article?id=10.1371/journal.pone.0091287
- http://news.nationalgeographic.com/news/2014/03/140313-new-species-dinosaurs-tyrannosaurus-rex-animals-science/

Qianzhosaurus sinensis

- http://www.nature.com/ncomms/2014/140507/ncom
  ms4788/full/ncomms4788.html
- http://www.nature.com/news/long-snouted-
  tyrannosaur-unearthed-1.15159

Spinosaurus aegyptiacus

- http://www.sciencemag.org/content/345/6204/1613.a
  bstract
- http://www.livescience.com/24120-spinosaurus.html

Torvosaurus gurneyi

- http://journals.plos.org/plosone/article?id=10.1371/j
  ournal.pone.0088905
- http://news.nationalgeographic.com/news/2014/03/1
  40305-dinosaurs-biggest-europe-torvosaurus-
  gurneyi-animals-science/

www.ingramcontent.com/pod-product-compliance
Lightning Source LLC
Chambersburg PA
CBHW052144220626
47052CB00005B/1182